SOCCER SHOOTOUT

BY JAKE MADDOX

illustrated by Sean Tiffany

text by Bob Temple

Librarian Reviewer
Chris Kreie
Media Specialist, Eden Prairie Schools, MN
MS in Information Media, St. Cloud State University, MN

Reading Consultant
Mary Evenson
Middle School Teacher, Edina Public Schools, MN
MA in Education, University of Minnesota

▼▼ STONE ARCH BOOKS
Minneapolis San Diego

Impact Books are published by Stone Arch Books
151 Good Counsel Drive, P.O. Box 669
Mankato, Minnesota 56002
www.stonearchbooks.com

Library of Congress Cataloging-in-Publication Data
Maddox, Jake.
    Soccer Shootout / by Jake Maddox; illustrated by Sean Tiffany.
    p. cm. — (Impact Books. A Jake Maddox Sports Story)
    Summary: When a new boy joins the Titans soccer team, Berk,
who has always played goalkeeper, is challenged for that position and he
must decide whether to hold a grudge or act for the good of the team.
    ISBN-13: 978-1-59889-844-6 (library binding)
    ISBN-10: 1-59889-844-2 (library binding)
    ISBN-13: 978-1-59889-896-5 (paperback)
    ISBN-10: 1-59889-896-5 (paperback)
    [1. Soccer—Fiction. 2. Teamwork (Sports)—Fiction.] I. Tiffany,
Sean, ill. II. Title.
PZ7.M25643So 2008
[Fic]—dc22   2007003635

Art Director: Heather Kindseth
Graphic Designer: Kay Fraser

1 2 3 4 5 6 12 11 10 09 08 07

TABLE OF CONTENTS

Chapter 1

SAVING THE DAY

Berk stood along the goal line. His heart was pounding in his chest so loudly that Berk wondered if the other players could actually hear it.

All around him, his teammates screamed for him. "Come on, Berk!" they yelled. "You can do it!"

Parents and friends stood on the sidelines of the soccer field. They, too, were yelling and cheering.

Berk danced back and forth on his feet, trying to stay calm. He wiggled his fingers a little to keep them loose.

The penalty kick he was about to face would decide the state championship. Berk always loved playing goalkeeper, but he never realized that the outcome of an entire season might be in his hands.

Berk's team had played a strong game. Peter Stanton, Berk's best friend, had scored the only goal for Berk's team, the Titans. It was a beautiful, curving shot from just outside the penalty area. But then, Peter always had a great shot.

That's partly how Berk got to be such a great keeper. Practicing with Peter and learning how to stop his shots had helped Berk improve his game.

Peter's goal had given the Titans a 1–0 lead early in the second half. With about ten minutes left in the game, the Cosmos had tied the score.

The Cosmos had a corner kick, and the player dropped the ball perfectly in front of the net. One of the Titans' defenders missed a chance to clear it, and a Cosmos player got a direct shot on goal.

Berk dove and stopped it, but the rebound went right to another player, who put it in the goal. Berk felt horrible, but the goal wasn't really his fault.

The rest of the game was close, but neither team had a great chance to score.

When the game ended in a tie, 1–1, it meant that a shootout would decide the winner.

Each team selected five players to hit penalty kicks against the other team's goalkeeper. Whichever team made the most goals would win the game.

Berk stopped the first two shots he faced, but the next two shots got past him. The first two Titans missed their shots, but the last three shooters all scored. Peter took the final shot and blasted it into the upper-right corner of the goal.

Now the Titans were leading the shootout, 3–2, and the Cosmos had only one shot remaining. If Berk stopped it, the Titans were state champions. If not, each team would have another shooter.

The referee approached Berk and reminded him of the rules. "Remember, you can't move forward until the ball is kicked," he said. Berk nodded.

Then, the ref turned to the shooter. "You can go on my whistle," he said. The boy nodded.

The Cosmos shooter was one of their best forwards. He was the boy who had scored their only goal of the game. He had tried two shots against Berk earlier in the game. Both times, he had tried to bend the ball toward the right side of the net. Would he do it again?

Berk bent at the knees. He put his hands up in the way his coach had taught him. All around him, people screamed. The noise didn't bother Berk. In fact, he was so focused on the play that he barely noticed.

The shooter placed the ball on the penalty-kick dot. He backed away from it, lining up his shot.

Berk felt a bead of sweat roll down his cheek. The other boy eyed the net.

As the two boys moved into place, the crowd fell silent. Finally, the referee's whistle broke the silence.

It was time.

Both players gathered themselves for a moment.

As the Cosmos shooter prepared to take his kick, Berk felt a surge of confidence rise up in his chest. This was it. The state title was on the line. He was ready.

The Cosmos shooter strode toward the ball. Berk had only an instant to try to determine which way he would shoot the ball.

Would he go right again, as he had before?

Berk started to lean that way. Then, as the boy's leg pulled back to take the shot, Berk could see what was happening. It looked like the boy was going to play the ball with the outside of his foot, pushing it toward Berk's left.

Berk timed his dive to the moment the boy made contact with the ball. Just as Berk expected, the boy pushed the ball toward Berk's left. Berk took a quick step that way and dove low, directly toward the spot the ball was headed.

It was a near-perfect shot. It was low and hard, heading for just inside the left goalpost.

But Berk's dive was right out of the goalkeeping textbook. His gloved left hand met the ball near the corner, pushing it out past the post.

No goal!

The Titans players leaped into the air and screamed. They rushed to the goal as Berk got back on his feet.

Berk had made the save!

All the players piled on him to celebrate their first state championship.

Chapter 2

ANOTHER PLAYER?

Summer turned to fall, and fall turned to winter. Berk and Peter played football in the fall. Berk played basketball in the winter, and Peter played hockey. But for both boys, these other sports were just to keep in shape. Soccer was their favorite sport.

When spring finally came and the snow began to melt, the boys began to start thinking even more about soccer.

Springtime meant tryouts and the start of another season.

It would be a chance for the boys to defend their state championship with the Titans.

Berk and Peter practiced indoors as much as they could. They would go to the gym after school, and Peter would practice shooting against Berk.

Berk couldn't dive to make stops on the hard gym floor, but he could work on his footwork and other skills.

One day, Berk arrived at school a little late. He strolled into his first class just before the bell rang.

He took his seat in the row nearest the door. As always, he glanced across the room at Peter and gave him a nod.

Peter had a strange look on his face. He seemed to want to tell Berk something. Berk furrowed his brow, then gave Peter a look that said, "What's up?" Peter tried to whisper something, but the teacher interrupted.

"Boys?" the teacher said. "Is there a problem?"

"Ah, no," Peter said. "Sorry."

For the rest of the period, the boys concentrated on their work.

When the bell rang to end the class, Berk waited for Peter by the door.

"What is it?" Berk asked. "What's going on?"

Peter turned to face his friend. "There's a new kid," Peter said.

"What? A new kid in school?" Berk replied.

"Yeah," Peter said. "And I guess he's a really good soccer player."

Berk thought about the comment for a minute. He wasn't sure what to say.

"Somebody said he was from down South, where they play all year round," Peter said.

Berk's face lit up. "Cool!" he said. "If he's really good, we'll win state again this year for sure!"

Peter didn't seem as happy. "Berk," he said. "You don't understand."

Berk stopped and looked back at Peter. He could tell something was wrong. Then, Berk figured it out. The new boy must be a forward.

Since Peter was a forward, too, he was probably worried about his playing time, Berk thought.

"Look, Pete," Berk said. "If he's a forward, there's no way he's as good as you are."

Peter shook his head. "No, Berk," he said. "That's not it."

"Then what?" Berk asked. "What can be so bad about a new kid who can play soccer?"

"Berk," Peter said. "The new kid is a goalkeeper."

Chapter 3

MEET THE NEW KID

Berk shrugged.

"So what?" he said. "I'm not worried. After all, I helped us win the state championship last year. It's not like Coach is going to replace me just because some new kid showed up."

Peter nodded. "Yeah, you're right," he said.

Berk wasn't nearly as confident as he was letting on.

Deep down, he was worried about the new boy.

All day long, other boys from his team were talking about the new kid.

"I heard he's six feet tall," one boy said.

"I heard he can boot the ball into the other team's goal," another said.

Berk knew the stories were ridiculous, but they were starting to bother him.

Finally, in sixth period, Berk got to meet the new boy.

Berk sat down in math class.

Just before the bell rang, the new boy walked into the room. He talked quietly with the teacher for a moment. Then he took a seat near the front of the room.

Berk was sitting two rows back.

The new guy was tall, yes, but he wasn't that tall. He seemed like he was probably a pretty good athlete, though.

When math class ended, Berk decided he should introduce himself. Berk approached the boy from behind and tapped him on the shoulder.

"Hey, I'm Berk," Berk said. "I hear you play soccer."

"Darn right," the boy said. "I'm Ryan. I hear you guys are good."

Berk chuckled. "Well, we won the state title last year," he said. "So yeah, we're pretty good."

Ryan shrugged his shoulders and rolled his eyes. "We won our championship, too," Ryan said. "And we play in a state where we take our soccer seriously."

Berk tried not to let the boy's comment get to him. "I think you might be surprised at how well we can play," he said. He let out a little laugh to try to ease any tension.

"I guess I'll find out at tryouts," Ryan said. "We'll see if any of you guys can score on me."

Berk paused. "Oh, so you're a keeper?" he said, pretending to act surprised. Ryan nodded. Berk paused for a moment, then said, "Me too."

Ryan looked him up and down. "Hmm," he said. "So I guess it's you against me at tryouts. Well, it's nice to know who the competition is."

"Yeah, it is," Berk replied. Now he was trying to act tough. But deep down, the other guy's confidence was getting to him.

Chapter 4

TRYOUTS

Berk used the few weeks remaining before tryouts to practice harder than he ever had. It was early spring and the snow was nearly gone. Berk convinced Peter to go out to the soccer fields behind school to practice with him.

They practiced close-in shots and long, curving shots. They practiced defending against corner kicks. They practiced penalty kicks and breakaways.

Berk practiced his punting, too. He wanted to make sure he was ready.

Finally, on the first day of tryouts, Coach Davis pulled Berk aside.

"Hey, Berk," the coach said. "How are you feeling about tryouts?"

"I'm ready," Berk said. "No worries."

Coach Davis smiled. "I'm sure you've met the new kid," he said. "Ryan looks like a good player. But I don't want you to worry."

Berk felt a huge sense of relief. The coach was telling him the job was his. But before Berk could relax too much, Coach Davis gave him a surprise. "I'm going to make sure the competition is as fair as possible," the coach said. "May the best player win."

The coach patted Berk on the back and trotted away.

"What?" Berk thought to himself. "Competition?"

Then Berk knew the game was on. He would have to play at his best in order to keep his job as the Titans' goalkeeper.

It didn't take long for the differences between Berk and Ryan to become clear during tryouts.

As they worked on various drills, Berk was clearly better at many of the technical parts of the game.

He made good decisions on when to come out of the goal to challenge a shooter or to pick up a loose ball. He always seemed to be in the right place at the right time.

When shots were taken on him, Berk made solid saves and controlled the rebounds.

Ryan was a little wilder in the goal. He took unnecessary chances, coming out of the net to challenge a player when it would have been smarter to stay back. He often found himself out of place.

But Ryan was a better athlete than Berk. So he often covered for his own fundamental mistakes by making spectacular diving saves.

Ryan could punt the ball much farther than Berk, but Berk's kicks were more on target to a teammate.

On the second-to-last day of tryouts, Coach Davis broke the Titans into two teams for a scrimmage.

The teams were pretty evenly matched. Berk was in one goal, Ryan was in the other. Peter was on Berk's team.

Before the scrimmage, Peter ran up to Berk. "Don't worry, buddy," he said. "I'll score on him and then you'll have the keeper job."

At first, the scrimmage was going just as the drills had gone. Berk was always in the right place.

When any shots were taken at him, Berk was ready, so the saves were pretty easy to make.

Ryan was running all over the field. At one point, he charged a forward who had the ball in the corner. That left the whole goal wide open, so the forward lofted a pass toward Peter.

Peter met the pass in the penalty area. He controlled the ball with his left foot, then blasted it with his right toward the open net. But Ryan's quickness allowed him to get back to the net. He dove across to his right and deflected Peter's pass toward the right post.

Another forward pulled the rebound in on the right side of the net.

Again Ryan charged, and the forward put the ball out front.

This time Peter tried to redirect the ball toward the left post. He didn't aim it perfectly, and Ryan dove back on top of the loose ball.

Berk's heart sank. He knew that if the same play had happened to him, neither of those shots would have been taken.

He would have stopped the first pass, and the play would have been over. But Ryan's wild style allowed him to make two spectacular-looking saves. Even Coach Davis was clapping and yelling.

Neither team scored in the scrimmage. Afterward, Coach Davis called Berk over to the sideline. "Berk," he said. "I have an idea."

Idea? Berk wasn't sure what to say.

Then the coach continued: "Have you ever thought about playing another position?"

Chapter 5

NEW POSITION?

Berk decided to be honest with his coach.

"Um, no, Coach," he said. "I've always wanted to be a goalkeeper."

Coach Davis put his arm around Berk's shoulder.

"Well, you have such great footwork, and you're always in the right place at the right time," Coach Davis said. "I think you might make for a great sweeper."

The sweeper plays right in front of the keeper. He is often the keeper's most trusted teammate.

The sweeper helps protect the goalkeeper and clears away loose balls in front of the net.

It was a very important position, Berk knew. And since Michael Swenson, the boy who played it last season, had moved, the position was open.

Still, Berk wasn't interested in it. "I'd rather play keeper," he said.

"I know," Coach Davis said. "But I think I'm going to go with Ryan in goal."

Berk was shocked.

It had been a long time since he'd cried about anything to do with sports, but he felt like it now.

"You'll be the backup keeper," Coach Davis continued. "And you'll still play all the time, because you'll be the sweeper."

Berk managed to mutter something that sounded like "Okay," but he was still fighting back tears.

As the players left the field, he ran off ahead of the group.

He changed clothes quickly and got on his bike for the short ride home.

One more day of tryouts remained, but Berk already knew where he stood.

On the final day of tryouts, he didn't even bring his goalkeeper gloves to the field. He practiced the entire time with the defenders.

During a break, Peter ran up to Berk.

"What the heck are you doing?" Peter asked. "Why aren't you fighting for the keeper spot?"

"Coach told me yesterday," Berk said. He couldn't bear to look at his friend. He kept his eyes fixed on the ground. "I'm going to be the sweeper."

"That stinks," Peter said. "At least you'll be on the field all the time with me."

Berk smiled a little. Just then, Ryan ran over for a drink of water. He walked right up to the boys. Berk cringed as he prepared for Ryan to gloat.

"Hey, Berk," Ryan said. "You're a good keeper. I'm sorry tryouts didn't turn out the way you wanted."

Berk was sure Ryan didn't mean what he said. "Yeah," Berk said. "Whatever."

"It was a good competition," Ryan said. He held out his hand to Berk. "No hard feelings?"

Berk shook Ryan's hand for a quick second. "No hard feelings," he forced out. Ryan trotted away.

"What's up with that kid?" Berk said to Peter. "He's Mr. Cool one minute, then pretends to be nice the next."

Peter was sure he knew what was going on.

"He's just trying to butter you up," Peter said, "because he knows that all season you'll be protecting him."

Chapter 6

LET THE GAMES BEGIN

After just a few weeks of practice, the Titans were ready to begin their season.

It would be a long schedule. There were twenty-four league games, plus four weekend tournaments.

At the end of the regular season there would be playoffs.

Before the Titans' first game of the season, Coach Davis gathered the players around for a pep talk.

"Well, boys, we're ready for another great season," he began. "Last year, we won the state tournament. I know some things are different this year, but I think we can do it again. And we have a new opportunity this year. Whoever wins the state title this year will be invited to play in a national tournament!"

Now the players were pumped. They couldn't wait to get on the field.

When the game began, Berk felt strange. Playing as sweeper meant moving around the field a lot and doing things that he wasn't used to doing.

Still, he handled the position well, so Ryan didn't have much work at the net.

The Titans controlled play for most of the game.

Peter scored a goal late in the first half to give the team a 1–0 lead against their opponents, the Storm.

Early in the second half, the Storm became more aggressive. They kept putting pressure on the Titans' goal. Berk and the rest of the defenders were busy clearing the ball away.

Midway through the half, the Storm pushed the ball down into the left corner of the field. Ryan charged out of the net to challenge the forward. That left the net empty.

"Ryan!" Berk yelled. "Get back in the goal!"

It was too late.

A Storm player hit the ball into the middle of the field.

Berk couldn't get to it, and the Storm's center forward pounded the ball into the open net. Ryan dived, but couldn't reach the shot.

As Ryan dug the ball out of the goal, Berk walked over to him.

"Ryan, don't charge into the corners," he said, as nicely as possible. "You have to stay in the net. Let your defense handle the corners."

"Maybe you should have cleared that ball away," Ryan snapped back. "You made me look bad."

Berk turned and trotted back onto the field. Minutes later, the Storm had another chance from the corner. Ryan charged again, and again the ball was lofted over his head.

This time, Berk slid in front of the forward and knocked the ball away.

When the ball was cleared to the other end of the field, Berk turned back toward Ryan.

"See?" Berk said. "You have to stay in the goal. That time, I saved you!"

Chapter 7

A LITTLE HELP

The Storm and the Titans ended the game in a 1–1 tie.

The rest of the Titans' season was a lot like that first game.

Ryan made some great saves, but his poor fundamental play cost his team several goals.

The Titans were scoring as many goals as they had the year before, but they were giving up a lot more.

Peter led the team with sixteen goals, but instead of winning games 2–1 or 1–0, the Titans were losing 3–2 or tying 2–2.

After that first game, when Ryan didn't seem to like Berk's advice, Berk stopped giving it. He did his best job as sweeper, trying to protect Ryan. But he didn't offer Ryan any help in how to play goalkeeper.

The Titans were barely able to make the league playoffs.

Their season record of twelve wins, eight losses, and four ties put them in fourth place — the last playoff spot.

They would have to win two league playoff games and three state tournament games in a row in order to go to the national tournament.

It seemed very unlikely.

It took the whole season, but finally Coach Davis saw that Ryan's risky play was hurting the team.

After the last game of the regular season, he took Ryan aside for a private talk. Berk couldn't hear what they were saying.

When the talk was over, Coach Davis called to Berk.

Berk ran up to him.

"Berk, I think we need to make a change," Coach Davis said. "I'd like to put you back in goal for the playoffs."

Berk wasn't sure what to say. He glanced across the field and saw Ryan.

The tall boy was walking away slowly, his head held low.

"Are you sure?" Berk said. "Ryan's been playing there all year."

"It's not working out," Coach Davis said. "If we want to go to nationals, we need you in goal."

It was a huge compliment, and Berk knew it.

Still, he felt uneasy. "Um, thanks, Coach," he finally said.

As the coach walked away, Peter approached. "I heard the great news!" he yelled. "That's awesome!"

"Yeah, awesome," Berk mumbled. "So why don't I feel better?"

That night at home, Berk pulled out his goalkeeper gloves. He tried them on. This time, they felt a little funny.

Berk stared at the gloves, and things suddenly became clear.

That night, Berk phoned Peter and asked if he could meet at the soccer field.

"Trust me," Berk told his friend. "I have an idea."

Chapter 8

HELPING OUT

Berk walked over to Ryan's house. He rang the doorbell and waited.

He wasn't sure how Ryan would react to him coming over. After all, they weren't exactly friends.

Ryan came to the door. When he saw Berk, he paused for a moment. Then he opened the door and stepped out.

"So, did you come over to gloat?" Ryan said.

"Not exactly," Berk said. "I have an idea."

Ryan looked confused.

Berk didn't worry about what he was about to say.

He decided direct honesty was the only way.

"Look, you make better saves than I do," Berk said. "But you're not a better goalkeeper than me."

"So you did come over to gloat," Ryan shot back.

"Just listen," Berk replied. "If we put our skills together, we'd have an awesome goalkeeper. So that's what we need to do."

"Huh?" Ryan said. "What are you saying? Are you nuts?"

"We need to combine our skills into one keeper," Berk said. "I'll never be able to make some of the amazing saves you make, because you're a better athlete than I'll ever be. But you can learn how to play goalkeeper as well as I do."

It was all becoming clear to Ryan. "So, you're going to help me with the fundamentals?" he said.

"Exactly," Berk said.

* * *

Throughout that weekend, Berk and Peter drilled Ryan on the fundamentals.

They worked on helping Ryan decide when to charge and when to stay in the goal. They even worked out a series of signals that Berk could give to Ryan to help him hold his place.

It wasn't easy, but Ryan was starting to get it.

* * *

At the next practice, Berk and Ryan approached Coach Davis together.

They presented their idea, and told the coach what they had already done.

Coach Davis seemed pleased.

"I'm not sure if this will work," he said. "But I'm proud of you boys for working together to solve this problem. Let's do it!"

Chapter 9

PLAN IN ACTION

It wasn't always smooth, but the plan worked.

Berk shouted "Goal!" whenever Ryan needed to stay put, and "Now!" when he needed to charge.

After a few games, Berk didn't need to make the calls anymore.

Ryan was figuring it out on his own.

Ryan kept making spectacular saves.

This time the saves were keeping the Titans ahead instead of covering up Ryan's own bad decisions. It made playing goalkeeper much easier.

The Titans easily advanced through the league playoffs and the first two rounds of the state tournament.

In the state championship, they again faced the Cosmos, just as they had the year before. This was it, their chance to go to nationals for the first time ever.

The Cosmos were a great team, and they had a powerful offense. That was clear in the first half, when the Cosmos pressured the Titans' goal.

Berk and the rest of the defense kept the ball away from the goal for most of the half.

Ryan made a few saves, too, and did a great job of playing the position fundamentally.

Early in the second half, Berk intercepted a pass at the top of the penalty area.

Looking ahead, he heard Peter yell "Send it!" as he took off down the sideline. Berk booted the ball high down the field, ahead of Peter.

With his speed, Peter beat the defense and controlled the pass.

He closed on the Cosmos goal and boomed a heavy shot toward the far upper corner.

As the ball hit the webbing of the net, Berk and the rest of the Titans yelled.

They were ahead!

Now they only needed to protect their lead. Against the Cosmos, it wasn't going to be easy.

Throughout the rest of the half, the Cosmos pressured the goal. Like many teams, they tried to advance the ball to the corners, then cross it into the middle of the field.

Ryan never budged on those plays. He was able to intercept several crossing passes as a result.

In the final minute, the Cosmos made one last rush up the field. They moved the ball into the corner, and a Titans defender rushed to challenge.

Berk moved to cover a player. But with the game on the line, the Cosmos brought more players into the zone.

The Titans defenders couldn't cover them all.

The Cosmos player kicked the ball toward the front of the goal.

Ryan froze. Berk could tell he was trying to decide if he should run out to try to play it or if he should stay in the goal.

Ryan stayed put. He saw the ball going toward an unguarded player near the penalty-kick dot.

Ryan prepared for the shot. He crouched low and kept his hands ready.

When the ball bounced off the player's foot, Ryan was ahead of it.

His sprawling dive met the ball perfectly. And, instead of knocking it away, Ryan caught it. He clutched it tightly as time expired.

The Titans were champions again!

Peter and Berk rushed to their keeper. Ryan still held the ball to his chest.

"You did it!" Berk yelled. "You did it!"

Ryan looked him in the eye. "No, we did it," Ryan said.

About the Author

Bob Temple lives in Rosemount, Minnesota, with his wife and three children. He has written more than thirty books for children. Over the years, he has coached more than twenty kids' soccer, basketball, and baseball teams. He also loves visiting classrooms to talk about his writing.

About the Illustrator

When Sean Tiffany was growing up, he lived on a small island off the coast of Maine. Every day, from sixth grade until he graduated from high school, he had to take a boat to get to school. When Sean isn't working on his art, he works on a multimedia project called "OilCan Drive," which combines music and art. He has a pet cactus named Jim.

Glossary

competition (kom-puh-TISH-uhn)—a contest, or a situation in which two or more people all want the same thing

fundamentals (fuhn-duh-MEN-tuhlz)—basic and necessary skills

gloat (GLOHT)—to show happiness that someone else has failed

penalty kick (PEN-uhl-tee KIK)—in soccer, an extra shot awarded against a team that has committed an offense

position (puh-ZISH-uhn)—the role assigned to a player

rebound (REE-bound)—to bounce the ball back into play

scrimmage (SKRIM-ij)—a game played for practice

More About Soccer Positions

A soccer team is made up of eleven players: forwards, midfielders, defenders, and a goalkeeper.

The forwards are responsible for most of the team's scoring. Since they play in front of the rest of the team, they can take the most shots.

Midfielders play directly behind the forwards. They help with ball control and passing.

The defenders are next in line. They keep the other team's players from scoring.

Finally, the goalkeeper prevents shots from crossing the goal line.

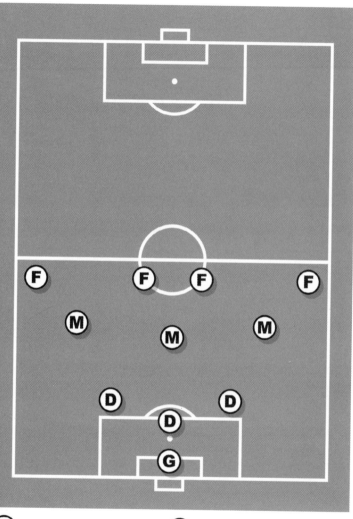

F -Forwards (3-5 Players) **D** -Defenders (2-4 Players)

M -Midfielders (3-4 Players) **G** -Goalkeeper

Discussion Questions

1. Why do you think Ryan acted the way he did when he first got to the new school?

2. Berk could have made Ryan look bad by letting other teams get good shots on him. Instead, Berk tried his best to protect Ryan. Why?

3. Coach Davis offered Berk a chance to be the goalkeeper again. Why do you think Berk felt funny about that?

Writing Prompts

1. At the beginning of the book, Berk faced a situation in which the game was up to him. Write about a time when you had a lot of pressure on you, and how you handled it.

2. Have you ever been replaced by someone else, like Berk was? Write about how that felt.

3. At the end of the book, Berk did something to help out Ryan. Write about a time when you helped someone achieve something great.

OTHER BOOKS

JAKE MADDOX

SNOWBOARD DUEL

STONE ARCH *Realistic Fiction*

Hannah and Brian have the run of Snowstream, a cool winter resort. But a new kid, Zach, starts a boys-only snowboard cross team. What will Brian do when he's forced to choose between Hannah and snowboarding?

BY JAKE MADDOX

Best friends Carlos and Ricky race all the time, but when their bikes are sabotaged before a major race, they can't trust each other. They'll have to band together to figure out who's pulling a double-cross.

Internet Sites

Do you want to know more about subjects related to this book? Or are you interested in learning about other topics? Then check out FactHound, a fun, easy way to find Internet sites.

Our investigative staff has already sniffed out great sites for you!

Here's how to use FactHound:

1. Visit *www.facthound.com*

2. Select your grade level.

3. To learn more about subjects related to this book, type in the book's ISBN number: **1598898442**.

4. Click the **Fetch It** button.

FactHound will fetch the best Internet sites for you!